But just as he was about to give them a shake Little Pip saw a note . . .

And the note said . . .

Little Pip studied the note and tried to remember
what was SO special about today . . .

"Maybe it's my birthday?"
he grinned.

"Or . . . Christmas!
YIPPEEEE!"

But, no, neither of these things
sounded quite right.

In the end, there REALLY was only
one way to find out . . .

"Wake Up, Daddy Grizzle!"

Daddy Grizzle sat up with a sudden start,
    and the first of the day's many questions began . . .

"*D*addy Grizzle!" said Little Pip.
"What IS so special about today?"

"Well . . ." began Daddy Grizzle,
but before he could explain further
Little Pip shouted,

"WAIT!"

For suddenly Pip had noticed that the special day
was something to do with . . .

DADDY GRIZZLE

and now he wanted to remember
what it was all by himself!

"Can I have just one enormous
clue?" he begged.

"Well," said Daddy Grizzle. "Last night, after we'd hung up the banner, we planned a WHOLE DAY OUT to celebrate my special day. And the first thing we decided to do was find some sticks!"

"Sticks?" repeated Little Pip.
(It wasn't much of a clue, but it was all he had . . .)

And while Little Pip pondered on "sticks",
there was a knapsack to pack,
and some treats to be found,
then - HuRRAH -
they were ready to go!

So out they went into the bright, sunny woods,
with the birds singing and the brook babbling,
to see how many sticks they could find.

After they'd collected a whole heap of sticks
Little Pip remembered something else . . .

"A campfire!"
he shouted.

"But can you remember **where** we planned to build our campfire?" asked Daddy Grizzle, giving his nose a HUGE exaggerated rub.

"*I* do remember!" gasped Little Pip.
"Big Bear Island!"

"That's right!" cheered Daddy Grizzle.
"That's EXACTLY where we planned to go!"

But, oh dear, now there was
something **else** they BOTH had to remember.

Hmmm . . . where **had** Daddy Grizzle left their boat?

*T*hey found it eventually.

"It's over here!" called Pip.

only stopping to wave at their friends – "Hello!" –

Then they rowed down the splish, splosh river,

splash!

"Tee hee!"

and dip their toes in the water – "It tickles!"

And when they reached Big Bear Island
they quickly jumped ashore and found the
perfect place to make a campfire.

BUT . . .

"Oh dear," sighed Little Pip.
"We've got nothing to cook on the fire."

"Yes we have!" said Daddy Grizzle.
"Look what I remembered to bring . . ."

"Marshmallows!"

"Yippeeee!"
shouted Little Pip.

"Today must be a VERY special day if we're having marsh-uh-oh!" Suddenly Little Pip remembered EVERYTHING!

"Daddy Grizzle," he said very quietly.
"I've just remembered what's SO special about today . . .

It's the day when all
the woodland creatures
give their daddies a special day
to thank them for all the
lovely things they do."

"THAT'S IT!" cheered Daddy Grizzle.
"I knew you'd remember.
Well done, my Little Pip!"

But instead of looking pleased
Little Pip looked sad.

"Daddy Grizzle," he sighed.
"I've forgotten to make you a card
OR give you a present!"

"Oh, don't worry!" said Daddy Grizzle. "We can make a card when we get home. And you've already given me a **wonderful** present . . .

a day out doing all the things I like to do most - rowing down the river, building a fire - and, best of all, spending some time with my **favourite** little bear cub in the whole wide wood . . . YOU!"

Little Pip gave a BIG happy shrug, and said,
   "One day, when I'm bigger, I'm sure I'll be much better
at remembering. But there's one thing I know I'll NEVER forget . . ."

   "And what's that?" asked Daddy Grizzle.

"*I*'ll never forget how much
I love you, Daddy Grizzle!"

The rest of their special day was spent playing in the sunshine . . .

HuUUuchZzzz^z...

and catching up on some
   much needed "Daddy" sleep . . .

HuUUuchZzzz_z...

until Daddy Grizzle woke up
   and noticed something drifting
   down the river . . .

Bear Mallows

"Little Pip, before we go home I think we should build ourselves a raft!"

"But why?" asked Little Pip.

Daddy Grizzle gave a BIG bear chuckle . . .

"Because your dear old Daddy Grizzle forgot to tie up the boat!"

the end

For Goldy and all her sprinklings of magic! – M. S.

For Goldy indeed, and all the little Beaver Scouts,
especially those of Wotton-under-Edge – S. B.

BZZZ BZZZ BZZZ...

PUFFIN BOOKS
Published by the Penguin Group: London, New York,
Australia, Canada, India, Ireland, New Zealand and South Africa
Penguin Books Ltd, Registered Offices: 80 Strand, London WC2R 0RL, England
puffinbooks.com
First published 2015
001
Text copyright © Mark Sperring, 2015
Illustrations copyright © Sébastien Braun, 2015
All rights reserved
The moral right of the author and illustrator has been asserted
Made and printed in China
ISBN: 978–0–723–29570–9